for Elijah
who's the point of it all

About This Book • The illustrations for this book were hand-drawn and painted in watercolor, then composited and rendered digitally. This book was edited by Megan Tingley and Anna Prendella and designed by Karina Granda. The production was supervised by Erika Schwartz, and the production editor was Jen Graham. The text was set in Mrs Eaves, and the display type is KG Second Chances Solid.

HOW TO POTTY TRAIN YOUR PORCUPINE

Tom Toro

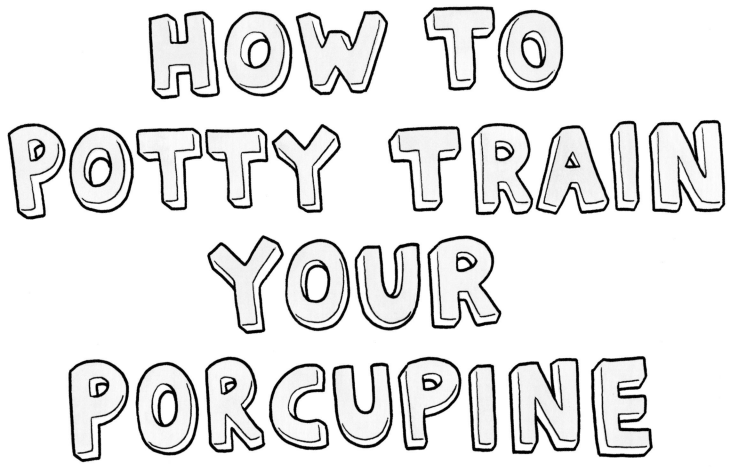

L B

Little, Brown and Company
New York Boston

Our parents will let us keep the porcupine
if she doesn't make a mess.

But diapers don't work,
for obvious reasons.

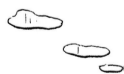

And it turns out she can't share
the litter box with our cat.

The backyard isn't a good spot because
the porcupine needs her privacy.

We try putting newspapers
on the kitchen floor,

but she keeps getting preoccupied.

So there's only one thing left to do....

POTTY TRAIN

THAT PORCUPINE!

But first we need to procure some
prickle-proof protection.

And then we need to find her.

Luckily for us, porcupines love music.

Unluckily for us, porcupines are fancy dancers.

But all that twirling makes
her hungry for a porcupine's
favorite treat—

CHIPS!

She loves chips so much, she doesn't even notice as…

...we shampoo and condition her quills...

...use our mom's hair curlers
so the porcupine won't poke us...

...and then put her on the potty with a gentle pat-pat.

We did it!

Whoops.

Maybe the curlers were a mistake.

Now what can we do?

We'll never get to keep the porcupine for a pet.

Maybe all we need to do is ask her nicely?

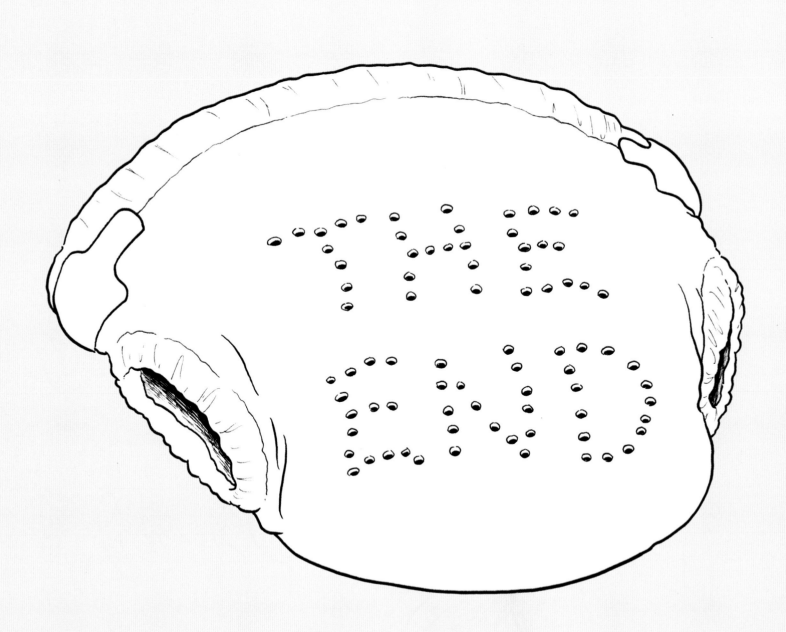